TODAY

Nora

WILL BE A

PRINCESS

Andrews McMeel
Publishing®

a division of Andrews McMeel Universal

PRINCESS
Nora

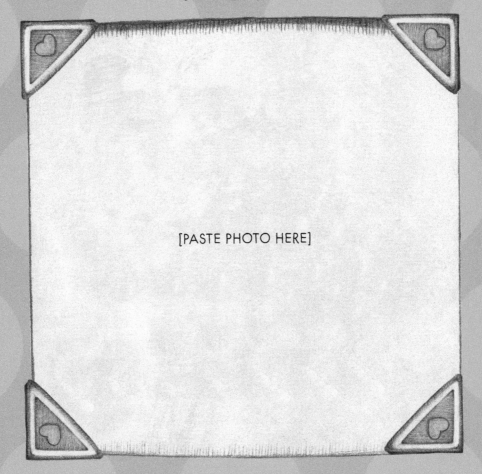

[PASTE PHOTO HERE]

FULL NAME: _____

AGE: _____

Nora,

this book is for you!

FROM: _____

MESSAGE: _____

_____

_____

Today,
Nora
will be a princess.

She'll get to wear
pretty dresses
that swish
and swirl . . .

and
sparkly shoes
that make her
feel fancy.

Nora
will ride in
a royal carriage
wherever
she goes . . .

and wear
the most
beautiful
crown covered
with jewels.

But, mommy
says princesses
don't get
to play in
the mud.

Maybe
Nora
will be
a princess
tomorrow . . .

PRINCESS
Nora's
FAVORITE THINGS

COLOR: _____

FOOD: _____

GAME: _____

ANIMAL: _____

SONG: _____

MOVIE: _____

DRAW PRINCESS Nora

Andrews McMeel Publishing
a division of Andrews McMeel Universal
1130 Walnut Street, Kansas City, Missouri 64106

www.andrewsmcmeel.com

Library of Congress Control Number: 2014946447

Written by Paula Croyle
Illustrated by Heather Brown

CPSIA information can be obtained
at www.ICGtesting.com
Printed in the USA
LVHW071136170920
665299LV00057B/658

9 781524 847661